I0738855

Elephant's Kitchen

Elephant's Kitchen
An Aspergirl's Study in Difference

Stephanie C. Fox, J.D.

QueenBeeBooks

Bloomfield, Connecticut, U.S.A.

Copyright © August 2004
by Stephanie Carole Fox

All rights reserved. Published in the United
States by QueenBeeBooks, Connecticut.

This is a work of fiction. Any similarity to
persons living or dead is purely coincidental.

Library of Congress Cataloging-in-
Publication Data
Name: Fox, Stephanie C., author.
Title: Elephant's Kitchen – An Aspergirl's
Study in Difference / Stephanie C. Fox.
Description: Connecticut: QueenBeeEdit
Books, [2004].
Identifiers: ISBN 978-0-9996395-6-6
(paperback)
Subjects: 1. General—Fiction. 2.
Psychological—Fiction. 3. Short Stories
(single author)—Fiction.

www.queenbeeedit.com

Cover design by Stephanie C. Fox
Cover art by Stephanie C. Fox
Printed in the United States of America

Also by Stephanie C. Fox

The Book of Thieves

The Bear Guarding the Beehive

Scheherazade Cat:
The Story of a War Hero

An American Woman in Kuwait

Nae-Née
Birth Control: Infallible, with
Nanites and Convenience for All

Vaccine: The Cull – Nae-Née Wasn't Enough

New World Order Underwater:
The Nae-Née Inventors Strike Back

What the Small Gray Visitor Said

Almost a Meal –
A True Tale of Horror

Hawai'i – Stolen Paradise:
A Travelogue

Hawai'i – Stolen Paradise:
A Brief History

This story is dedicated to girls and boys who
grow up undiagnosed with Asperger's.

Asperger's is a wonderful condition that occurs
in a small percentage of the human population.
Contrary to what many neurotypicals say, it is
not a disorder. It is actually a minority model of
normal" humans.

Many famous people who have done
wonderful things have had Asperger's:
Marie Curie, Temple Grandin, Thomas Jefferson,
Wolfgang Amadeus Mozart, Jane Austen, Virginia
Woolf, Nikola Tesla, and many others.

Asperger's makes a person
different from the majority.

Asperger's leads to innovation,
invention, creativity,
and even stardom.

It's a stardom of a very
different and unique sort.

Elephant's Kitchen
– An Aspergirl's Study in Difference

Every Sunday, my family attended St. Anne's Church. My parents liked to see other families at the church, and chat with them and the minister after the service. My mother liked to see her friends; my father just went to please her. As far as he and I were concerned, it was the pipe organ and the concerts that made going there worthwhile.

We weren't religious; we liked to see the stained glass windows and carved wooden pews, and the stone masonry was beautiful, but the sounds that the pipe organ made when visiting artists were invited made the tedium of the services seem pointless. We didn't need a lecture on how to be good people. But my mother insisted on attending and on listening to Mr. Baker, the minister. The service always included a sermon containing such good advice as "Do unto others as you would have others do unto you."

I could relate to that, and on both sides of the issue. That meant that I wouldn't be cruel to anyone, but if anyone were cruel to me, there would be payback. One part of religion that I disagreed with was the "turn the other cheek" doctrine. The problem with that was that more often than not, I had to do comply with it simply because I couldn't come up with an equally unyielding phrase to back up doing the opposite of that. Only recently, in a movie, had I heard "proportionate response" – the ideal comeback.

This past week at the exalted Havermeyer School, the exclusive private institution that I attended (conveniently located in the next town, so that my parents had to drive me there), Katie Wills and her clique had harassed me several times.

She was a bully, and the leader of her pack of idiots. Of course, they didn't seem like idiots when they spoke to teachers and most of the other kids, either girls or boys. They always knew how to come across as cool and up on the latest trends.

And that was why I didn't seem cool; I just didn't consider trends to be worthy of my attention, and they knew it. I also wasn't interested in bothering with Katie's nonsense, which was, according to my father, why she kept it up.

She and Amy and Erin had run around the halls when the teachers weren't in the immediate vicinity, making noise and messing with anyone they could. I was hard to get to, but not impossible; I couldn't focus my attention on my surroundings every moment. Katie knew that when she led her group past me and deliberately crashed into me as I was carrying my violin case, my sheet music, and slinging my book-bag over my shoulder. The sheet music went cascading down the stairwell in the academic building as I protected the violin, and the gang of bullies ran off, laughing hysterically.

I gathered my stuff up, organized it, and zipped it into my bag before moving on.

But once I had everything stashed in my locker in time for play practice, I was ready to move with more stealth and care. And I wouldn't head out of the music room again without gathering and packing every last thing – that was for sure.

Katie had a part in the play too. We were doing *The Merchant of Venice*, and I was Portia, the lawyer. She was my sidekick and servant, Nerissa. Maybe that bothered her. Katie had been in this private school with me since we were little, and had always sensed that I was a bit different and bullied me. I tried to stay away from her.

The drama teacher, Ms. Hathaway (that really was her name, and she even got teased about it by the headmaster, considering what she taught), had complimented me on my dress later that same day.

The dress had deep pockets, a beautiful floral pattern, three-quarter-length sleeves, and a roomy skirt. I had lots of them; my grandmother made them for me. Ms. Hathaway was looking for ways to save on costumes, and she thought that my grandmother's creations were almost exactly what the production needed.

Before I knew it, my grandmother – my mother's mother, whom I called Nana – had agreed to make the costumes for the play, and she was having a wonderful time.

So was I; Nana let me choose whatever colors I wanted for my dress.

Katie was less thrilled. She liked faddish stuff, uncomfortable outfits that were tight and had no pockets, and had derisively commented and mocked the beautiful clothes I wore for years. I thought it was hilarious that now she would have to wear them too.

She cornered me in the props area after Ms. Hathaway got my grandmother's phone number from me that afternoon and said, "Delphine, are you, like, happy that you wear theater costumes, like, all the time?" Amy and Erin appeared behind her like the sycophantic and obliging shadows that they were, snickering.

This was the part that I usually hated most – not knowing what to say until hours later and then regretting the lost moment. But that afternoon, I surprised myself.

"You mean, like, how you can't deal with the fact that, like, you can't always think of the next word in your sentence at like, the exact moment that it would be smooth to speak it?" I retorted.

Katie's face fell, and she hissed, "You stupid bitch!"

She lunged towards me then, but saved herself nicely as Ms. Hathaway appeared, pretending that she had tripped.

Ms. Hathaway gave the three of them a funny look and sent them off to set up for the next scene. I looked at her, carefully keeping my expression neutral. What had she heard? If she had heard it all, was she disgusted with me? She surprised me by smiling and telling me to please make a list of names, roles being played, and costume ideas for her and my grandmother to consider.

I had stood there, relieved and amazed, and nodded. Nana arrived at the end of the day to talk to the teacher and pick me up, and I had the list ready. When I went to get my things from my locker, I carefully checked the halls, but Katie was gone for the day.

As we rode to Nana's house (my parents were out for dinner with friends), Nana talked excitedly about all of the costumes she would be making. She was in her element, and wanted me to pick out whatever fabric I liked best from her collection before dinner.

Katie wasn't going to like that. Nana had the measurements of all of the girls, and I was the only one who would be able to choose my clothes. It must have been tough for a clothes horse like Katie, but for once, even though I expected more grief at school over this, I was excited and enjoying this.

Memorizing lines came naturally to me. This play was going to be great fun. I had tried out for play after play, but this was my first big role. That hadn't surprised me; the other kids had to have their chance too. But maybe, after the teachers saw what I could do, I would get another big role before graduation. This was my sophomore year.

I knew I didn't fit and I didn't care. Of course, if fitting in meant becoming adept at being mean – and being the first in an interaction to be mean – then that was just fine. Let them think I'm anti-social, even if I was merely asocial. The people who say that are really describing themselves anyway, so why should I care what they think?

Such a lot of effort it was, it seemed, to expend time and energy on figuring out how to deal with people. I couldn't expect to just copy one person's method of handling a particular situation; it would be necessary to ask several people and then come up with my own way. And then I would have to do this over and over again for each potential situation, and file the data away for random use whenever it was needed again! What a time-suck; I could be studying, but no – I had to learn social skills by rote and store them as data. Surely most people didn't have to spend time on this. Not me, and I wanted to study and practice the violin. Damnit.

Nana understood this. She didn't go to church anymore except for the organ recitals because her friends had either died or moved away, except for one who was Jewish and another who was Hindu, so she wouldn't need church to see them anyway.

I wished I could see Mrs. Srivashti more often, but high school and violin lessons took up most of my time. I missed going with Nana on Sunday evenings to eat her delicious, spicy food. Nana's food was delicious – I loved French recipes – but I kept thinking that if I could get my Sundays back, I could go with her again, and Mrs. Srivashti could show me her sitar again, and play something on it.

This was what I thought about as I listened to Mr. Baker talk on and on.

Yes, we ought to do unto others as we would have them do unto us – great thought – but I was all for retaliation if that would dose some bully with a taste of her own medicine. The last time I had done that – shown a bully what happens when you do nastiness and cruelty unto me – we had been eight years old.

Katie had invited me to her sleepover party. I woke up with a huge chunk of hair in the back missing, and with Katie and Amy and Erin grinning, waiting for me to notice. I didn't notice until I went to the bathroom, but after crying briefly, I noticed something else: scissors. There they were, carelessly forgotten on the sink counter.

When I came out, I threw my stuff into my bag and waited for the others to move on to the next bit of fun on the agenda. I tied my hair up in a clip, camouflaging the damage, got dressed, and bided my time. There were at least fifteen other girls at the party, and some of them had looked appalled at what had happened to me, but the deed was done, so after I had accepted a couple of expressions of sympathy, that was that. Soon Mrs. Wills was serving breakfast with the help of her live-in maid. Katie left for a moment to get something to show her friends, and I slipped out after her, moving as quietly as I could.

I followed, more terrified that I would be noticed and unable to exact revenge than anything else. But I was in luck; Katie stood over her box of Barbie doll clothes, rummaging, unaware that anyone else was there. Amy and Erin were eating downstairs. With Katie thus distracted, I came up behind her and pounced. Sitting on her, I grabbed half of her long, blond hair in one abrupt motion and chopped it off in the other. Now she had a crew cut on one side.

Justice.

My only regret was that I couldn't do Amy and Erin's hair also.

Abettors are as guilty as perpetrators, after all.

Katie had shrieked and cried as I cut her hair off, and then lunged at me as I leaped off, and I had run, skidding and almost falling halfway down, back to the kitchen.

Mrs. Wills had glanced up in confusion, then seen Katie's hair.

Her daughter had been thoroughly fleeced on one side.

And I was fully dressed, sneakers and all, picking up my overnight bag and pillow. She looked murderously at me, and I just unclipped my hair, showing her the missing part of my long, reddish brown hair. My heart was racing, but I felt good.

I told her I wanted to go home now.

She looked livid as she called my parents.

My mother looked livid too when she saw my hair.

Words were exchanged between Katie's parents and mine while I waited in the locked sanctuary of the car. It was nice to escape the harsh, heavy, sharp smell of Mrs. Wills' perfume. Dior, my mother told me it was; she herself wore a softer and sweeter scent that I liked much better (something by Chanel), and the next year I started wearing something soft and floral also – but not the same perfume. Something less expensive; we lived in rural Connecticut and I was a kid. What did I need Chanel for?

But back to the hair-cutting/fleecing incident…

I could hear Mrs. Wills raving that I was an evil, stealthy, treacherous little girl, and that she thought I should have given some warning about what I was about to do. That really infuriated me; Katie had attacked me as I slept with her friends watching. I had been the late-night entertainment. There was no reason for me to declare war. Katie had executed a sneak attack. It puzzled me that my retaliatory, unannounced response was viewed as an unfair attack. Also, what was the point of giving any warning at all? Stealth was the way to go. Announcing one's plans – or thoughts – was practically a guarantee of failure.

At first, my mother had been angry with me, but my father was so proud of me that she came around quickly. I refused to let her even my hair out, insisting upon clipping it into an updo until it grew out. She compromised by trimming it as it grew over the next few months, until finally I had a curtain of long, wavy hair that fell past my shoulders again.

Katie had had to wait longer, and she had come back to school with a pixie cut.

I didn't say anything to her about it.

As far as I was concerned, we were more than even.

That was probably why she didn't walk all over me, but I never trusted her.

That had been my mistake when I was little, and often still was with others.

I couldn't tell when someone was lying, or when they didn't really want to be my friend. If I had been able to do that, I would have seen that Katie had it in for me as part of the entertainment at that party.

After that, I had few friends, which I realized was nothing new. Party invitations mean nothing when all of the girls in the class received one. I chose social outcasts as friends from then on.

It was a semi-conscious decision. Boys would sometimes seem nice, and sometimes not. I didn't bother to have a boyfriend, but girls like Katie did. I found two nice friends at school who arrived the next year, Nicole and Ariel. Their parents weren't wealthy, and they didn't worry about the latest fashions or movie and TV personalities.

Nicole was bit plump, but not truly

overweight, while Ariel was stick thin.

Neither of them fitted in with the "in" crowd, but they both were able to intuitively understand how other kids thought. They were never at a loss as to how to handle a situation…unlike myself.

My last successful encounter with a bully had been six years ago, and every other one since then had been a study in awkwardness, delayed responses, and being mocked.

But there was nothing really wrong with me.

I got good grades, though they were all over the range (not just As, not just Bs, and there was always one C aside from gym class, which was always a C). Once a year, I entered a short story in the school magazine, *The Flying Broomstick*, and had it published. A couple of times I even won prizes. And I played the violin, got small roles in the plays, and sang in the Havermeyer Choir. I wished I were a soprano rather than an alto, but I kept this to myself. I liked the melody better than the harmony, and got lost sometimes trying to follow along.

"Why don't you go out with the kids and cheer for the field hockey team?" my mother would ask sometimes.

"I hate sports and noise," I would say.

My father never said anything about it; he just showed up with his camera for concerts and plays. He told me that he hadn't been athletic either. He had played the French horn all through high school and into college, until he went to the Wharton School. Then he was just too busy studying. He was satisfied with my decisions.

I didn't care that my social life wasn't full. I was satisfied with that too…

…except that I wanted quiet, and I wanted to continue working with more sleep.

Sometimes I was just so tired. I hated getting up early, but French homework took so long and I couldn't go to sleep without finishing ALL of my work. Get up early and do it?! No way; I had told my mother that I wouldn't be able to sleep worrying about it. I mean, how much time would I need to complete it? If I just stayed awake until it was finished, I would be sure to finish. At least she was proud of me for that; she said so.

Saturdays were my chance to catch up on sleep.

Sundays were wrecked with church.

I had to get out of that.

Going out with my parents was nice, but not when I was so tired and had a weekend's worth of studying and violin practice to do. High school was more work and took up more time than junior high school. Of course, that was the point; my parents wanted me to go to a good college, so they were sending me to the Havermeyer School from first through twelfth grades.

The trouble with that was that I liked it and put it ahead of socializing and any other demand on my time. Everything else was a drain on my time. I was tired, and I would not accept any changes in my routine that might compromise my academic life.

Routines were comforting and reassuring. Any change in them and I feared lower grades, entrapment by bullies, and who knew what else. I just wanted to get back to my room, my beautiful black cat, Phantasm, and my books and violin. Just knowing that I was back with my parents and that no distractions could get in to bother me made me calm and focused.

Night was the best time – no cabinet doors shutting, no toilets flushing, no sounds but my cat purring – I could really concentrate. Someday, I promised myself, I would be a writer with all degrees earned, quiet at night, and time to write. There would be a cat and a husband, but until then I was stuck in this rut.

A crying, shrieking, howling baby snapped me out of this reverie.

Why did people have to bring the little monsters to church?! At least at the movies it didn't happen as much; here it was a weekly occurrence. I couldn't focus on Mr. Baker's voice at all now. He had moved on to talking about specific good deeds that he had witnessed over the past week, but I couldn't concentrate on either his dull, inane speech or my own thoughts. All I wanted was for that noise to cease. I turned and watched until the door closed on the mother with the baby.

Then I faced front again, relaxing.

There was a Sunday School room that doubled as a room for crying babies.

My mother used to leave me in there when I was little to be read to and to play games. She would come back to find me sitting quietly on the side, observing everyone else in silence.

When I was twelve, she volunteered me to help with the younger kids.

That had lasted for a grand total of one day.

I was just as quiet as ever, and utterly clueless as to how to handle tantrums and other noise. When things got loud, I had moved to the side of the room again, leaving the adults to handle it. The noise in there with all of those little kids – the sustained level of constant loudness – numbed me. I lapsed into a wide-eyed stare at nothing, waiting for the hour and a half to end. There was that, and the fact that I moved out of reach whenever a toddler tried to touch my legs with sticky little hands.

Once, a little boy had leaned towards

me with chocolate cake all over his hands and tried to balance on me. I had darted away just in time not to let him get that mess all over my dress, and he fell forward. Screaming and crying came next, and with that, I was off the hook. The woman in charge, Mrs. Alistair, had looked askance at me. I had just looked back at her expressionlessly, like an inmate waiting for my time in there to end.

When it did, I left with relief, and was not asked back.

I never heard a word about it because of what I said to my mother when she came to get me, which I made sure to say loud enough for Mrs. Alistair to hear: "That had to be a carefully planned set-up on your part to stress me out and make me miserable and then call me selfish when I inevitably turned out not to want to deal with little kids."

The two of them had clearly gotten my blatant, sledgehammer of a hint.

When I got home, I had sat in my room for over an hour, still staring, petting Phantasm until I could think clearly again. The quiet was wonderful. I sat there so long that my parents each came upstairs to check on me, and I told them that I didn't like babies and little kids, and that I just wanted a husband and a cat when I grew up. My father didn't mind, but my mother looked worried. I told her that it would be unfair to a kid to have it unless I really wanted it and could handle it. She looked more accepting of the idea then.

It wasn't that I didn't want to do anything for anyone else.

I just hadn't figured out what, beyond helping the girl with the prosthetic leg up the icy steps in the dead of winter when no one else saw the fear in her eyes (no one else was even paying attention), that I could do. I cleaned things up, I helped with dishes every night, and I kept my room neat.

Maybe when I completed my formal education I would find something useful to do. But for now, I had to finish school and do well at it. I could worry about other things after that, when I was free – free of routines and able to sleep enough.

My facial expressions revealed so little that occasionally I was accused of selfishness by people at St. Anne's – which was another reason why I hated to go there much. Only my eyes widened when I felt stressed out. I couldn't expect to please everyone all of the time; better to just go to the organ recitals.

But I was still stuck. My mother wasn't ready to let me stay home on Sundays.

Today the service ended with its usual pleas for food to give to the poor at Elephant's Kitchen, which was what St. Anne's called the small house in the backyard of the church. Elephant's Kitchen was a cottage about half the size of my grandmother's house, with a big front room set up like a store where the women who ran it sat at a long table boxing up some of every type of food for the people who came to get it. The food was neatly organized by category in the back room, arranged on shelves with labels, and in the refrigerator.

At last church services ended and we got up.

I looked everywhere but into people's eyes, but I did respond as I had been taught whenever someone spoke to me, politely greeting them back. If I knew something about a person's family or interests, I asked about it, another skill that I had learned from my mother. It was important, and I knew it, but I had to force myself to do it.

If I didn't force myself, I would just stay lost in thought, and not bother to make eye contact with people. Looking people in the eyes didn't come naturally, and I couldn't read the expression in someone's eyes anyway. I just wanted to get back to my books.

As I stood in the huge stone doorway with my parents, spacing out and thinking about sitting with Phantasm and writing my history essay, I heard Mr. Baker asking my mother something.

"Hello Tom, Alyssa," he boomed (his voice was always too loud on Sundays, the same decibel whether he was in the pulpit or out of it), "Can you help me find another pair of hands to help Susan out in Elephant's Kitchen? There seem to be more people coming there lately, and they could use some more help."

He knew that my mother would never do that herself; it would mean lots of time with Mrs. Wills. Instead, my mother coordinated the supplies for the charity kitchen, communicating with local bakeries, coffee houses, and a gourmet grocery store to get donations. Mrs. Baker got shipments from the government in bulk. Susan Wills handed the food out to people who came in on Saturday mornings, along with other people who attended St. Anne's.

My mother didn't like Mrs. Wills. I figured that my exchange of unwanted coiffures with Katie had something to do with it and left it at that.

But I couldn't believe what happened next.

My mother glanced at Susan Wills, who was chatting with some people over by the steps to the organ seat (that was upstairs, above the front door), and back to Mr. Baker. Then she spoke.

"I would love to, but I have music lessons to teach on Saturdays from 10a.m. throughout the day. Maybe Delphine could help you – what is it, 9:30 to 11:30 on Saturday mornings?"

The minister looked at me. I would have given anything to be elsewhere at that moment. Saturday was my one day to sleep in. I certainly didn't want to spend it with the mothers of my bullies, several of whom stood chatting in the yard.

"Well, Delphine, how about it? Will you help us? See how the have-nots look?"

Saying no to the minister was, of course, out of the question. "Sure. I'll see you next weekend," I said.

"Great!" boomed Mr. Baker. "You'll learn lots!" And with that, he turned to the next family exiting the church.

Perfect, I thought. Now I'm trapped. My routine is ruined, no sleep, and I'll be stuck with Mrs. Wills. I didn't know why she insisted upon running the distribution in Elephant's Kitchen anyway. She wasn't nice, and helping poor people seemed like a task for nice people, not unpleasant ones.

Why didn't anyone else see that?

And why was it that I could see that, but I couldn't read most other people?

And why did my mother have to volunteer me for this?! Was it out of some sense of bourgeois guilt? Did she feel bad about being well-off, and want to make sure that I didn't take my situation for granted? If so, fine – I would take a good look at the poor people and see how bad things could be. I was already worried about the future; my parents were rich, not me. I had to sell whatever I wrote in the future, or I could be in big financial trouble. Unlike the people in movies and sitcoms about twentysomethings, I didn't look forward to living on my own one bit. It was just another anxiety-inducer.

My parents were as wealthy as any of the other Havermeyer School parents, but my mother had come from a middle class family, and I knew that my father's parents had cut him off when he married her. They had wanted him to find a wealthy snob at their country club, but he found his best friend instead, and had married her. That was why I had never met them, but knowing what I knew, I didn't mind. They sounded like awful, controlling individuals. My father had gone on to make his own millions with his own financial planning business, and had little contact with his own family since. I guess my parents were just determined that I would not be a snob.

Maybe if I had talked to them more,

they would have known that I was just as determined about that.

Oddly, now that I was slated to spend two hours per weekend with Mrs. Wills, my mother suddenly decided to share some information about her with me. She had never done that before. All I knew was that Susan Wills was snobby, she wore the latest styles from top-priced labels which she bought on weekly trips to Manhattan, she reeked of Dior, and she looked as though she had just stepped out of a high-end salon or spa. She was rumored to have been a New York City fashion model in her twenties, and had invested enough of her husband's pharmaceutical company profits in plastic surgery to look much the way she had at that time.

My mother surprised me at lunch by saying, "Delphine, I know you'd rather sleep on Saturday mornings. Let us know what it's like helping out at Elephant's Kitchen. Working there should really teach you what Mr. Baker talked about, but it should also be your choice once you've been there for a couple of months. Charity only counts as charity if you really want to give whatever you're giving. It should be done gladly and graciously, without judging the recipients, just like Mr. Baker said."

"Okay, Mom. Thanks. But why are you saying this?"

My mother went on, "Susan Wills is not a nice person, so I won't blame you if this doesn't work out. I'm about to tell you some things that I don't want you to repeat to anyone."

She waited for a moment, looking at me, so I said, "Okay, I won't."

Satisfied, my mother continued. "Susan Wills grew up around here, attending the best schools without studying much, continuing to attend on the strength of her family's influence in this area. Your father couldn't stand her, but she was interested in him. He didn't want someone who didn't appreciate how lucky she was – financially, I mean. Susan has always had the best of everything, and believes herself to be genuinely entitled to it. She doesn't speak to me unless she has to – she sees me as a usurper. I guess in a way I am a usurper – my parents weren't rich, but a guy she had her eye on wanted me rather than her."

This was the first time I had heard this

part about my parents' courtship; it had previously been more about my father's parents than about rivals. I listened with interest, and why not? This was the mother of nastiest girl I knew – like mother, like daughter.

But that was it; my mother concluded with, "Anyway, don't let her get to you – just do a good job at Elephant's Kitchen."

I promised that I would, ate my soup and salad and said I was going to finish writing a paper this afternoon. Then I went upstairs, where I spent the rest of the day writing and watching DVDs. While I watched the DVDs, I took notes for an outside writing project. I intended to write fiction when it wasn't outside of my academic schedule – novels, but not trashy romances – and I already did that on school vacations.

On Monday, during lunch with Nicole and Ariel, I told them what was going on.

Nicole looked up from an article she was preparing for the school newspaper, and said that I should just do it for a few weeks and then tell my parents I had to study.

Ariel, who had a lovely soprano voice that was the only thing about her that I envied, looked up from her Juilliard application and said I should add that I needed to practice the violin and get enough sleep.

Nicole grabbed the Juilliard brochures and swatted her with them, laughing. "You would say that! How many times are you going to practice writing your essay for that school?"

"Until I think I've written the one that will help me get accepted," Ariel said.

We told her for what might very well have been the hundredth time that Julliard would definitely take her, and that sophomore year was a bit early to start writing that essay. She sung precisely on key and worked hard at it, and was in a local group outside of school. She even took lessons with Mrs. Srivashti in raga songs, just to add depth and variety to her application.

I settled in for a week of less sleep, more anxiety, and dread of the coming Saturday. I was going to lose sleep and study time. And spend quality time with

Mrs. Wills. And meet people who had no choice about what they ate because they couldn't pay for it themselves. I hoped I could look them in the eye and not depress them further.

If I were poor and couldn't pay for food, I would still be a fussy eater. And I would probably be malnourished, because I wouldn't just eat whatever came my way. I hate that saying that beggars can't be choosers. Once, when I was in Manhattan with my parents overnight, I had been allowed to go around the corner from the hotel to buy a cup of hot chocolate, and a homeless woman asked me for something to eat from a deli. I invited her in there with me and insisted that she order whatever she wanted. She was a bit stunned, but the mere idea of getting something and assuming that she ought to just eat it and like it infuriated me. I wouldn't like that attitude directed at me!

Once again, I found myself wishing that I were done with my formal education, in control of my time and schedule, writing late at night when no one else was up – I was a night owl anyway – and with enough sleep not to get headaches. I could concentrate late at night with all of the distractions of daytime out of the way, dealt with, and being out of school would free me up to keep track of the news. I preferred to read it; I just got more out of it that way. But with homework to do, I had very little time left for that.

I wished there were a way to help people without this sort of direct interaction, but I wasn't sorry that I was about to do this. Any chance to learn something new, see something that I haven't seen before, and understand something that I would not otherwise appreciate, was welcome. What was not welcome was not knowing how long I would have to do it. I like to be able to see a beginning, a middle, and an end to a thing.

Our house was just a couple of streets away from St. Anne's and Elephant's Kitchen. It was a beautiful colonial one, surrounded by gardens of roses, irises, herbs and lilac bushes, though none of these were blooming just yet. The wisteria vines that crawled around the back door smelled wonderful now, though; spring had just sprung. I liked to sleep with my window open and smell their perfume as I lay in bed. I was probably going to miss that this spring.

On Saturday, I got up at eight-thirty and ate breakfast. As I got dressed, I thought, I wonder what the homes of the people who go to Elephant's Kitchen are like – or whether they even have homes. At least it was an hour and a half later than when I got up to go to school. I hoped that I could stay up writing late at night someday, with no worries about what time to get up the next morning. Every other thought of mine was about that lately, like a soothing mantra! But it kept my mind off of Elephant's Kitchen as I walked the two blocks through town to St. Anne's.

Mr. Baker was waiting for me outside. "Ready to serve the needy?" he asked. I noticed that his voice was lower than its usual Sunday decibel. Old-looking cars were inching near the new Mercedes and Saabs, with drivers looking as if they didn't want to be noticed. I wondered how people came to need free food.

"Yes, I am," I replied.

"Well, just go around to the side door there, and Mrs. Wills will explain what needs to be done." The minister turned to go.

"Um…Mr. Baker?"

"Yes, Delphine." He stood waiting, looking eager to get back to writing tomorrow's sermon.

"I was just wondering…why it's called Elephant's Kitchen." He probably thought I was wasting his time, procrastinating, but I really wanted to know.

But Mr. Baker just brightened up some more. "Excellent question! We call it that because an elephant never forgets a lesson, and the lesson here is that we should always be ready to help people who need help, if we possibly can."

I nodded politely. "Oh. That's very…appropriate, then," I said. "Well…thanks. I guess I'll see you tomorrow."

Mr. Baker smiled at me and went into his office.

Time to face the monster. I went to the side door of the cottage, glanced up at the cute, cartoonish elephant that was painted on the sign over the door, and went in. Sure enough, Mrs. Wills was to be found imperiously ordering her friends about as they lined up boxes and checked the food. Yeah…like mother, like daughter, I thought.

Mrs. Wills greeted me with a perfunctory smile and told me to take a seat at the end of the table. All of the seats faced the front door of the cottage. I gave her the bag of food that my mother had sent and went over to the table.

I sat down and noticed that the woman next to me was the same woman who made gourmet patisseries, mousses, and other fabulous Belgian treats at a shop down the street. "Hi, Ms. Sauvelle!" I said.

"Delphine – how are you? Call me Eleanor." She smiled at me.

"Okay, Eleanor – I'm okay, thanks." I smiled back. "So what do we do? How do we know how much of what to give people?"

"Oh, don't worry. You just ask how many people there are in their household, then give one of every category of food plus a few extras per person. It's easy, and you won't get fired…unlike the people who need the food."

"Hmm…is it okay if I look around the kitchen before it opens? I don't want to hold people up – I just thought I should see what's where."

Eleanor waved to Mrs. Wills, who had heard and nodded back.

I got up and looked around at the assortment of bags of sliced wheat bread, gourmet coffee, random gourmet items such as fancy chocolate bars and brand-name sauces from nearby specialty shops, U.S.D.A. packages of nonfat dry milk and walnuts, etc. "NOT TO BE SOLD OR EXCHANGED," said those bags. Great, I thought – imagine having a visitor to one's home see that. Self-confidence had its limits; who could refrain from being ashamed of needing this kind of help? I went back to my seat next to Eleanor Sauvelle.

At precisely ten o'clock, Mrs. Wills unlocked the door. Everyone knew exactly what time it was, because Mrs. Wills made quite a performance of checking the time and announcing that the door would remain unlocked for exactly, precisely one hour and not a minute more. The first people to arrive looked alarmed at this pronouncement, as if they expected her to slam the door in their faces on the spot.

I noticed that Mrs. Wills and her friends all glared at the people who came in and looked them each up and down, as if sizing them up for a slaughterhouse. It felt embarrassing just being there. I got up early for this?

At eleven o'clock there were still some people there, and Mrs. Wills wasted no time in locking the door. Eleanor was still smiling and handing out food. She never glared at anyone. I made up my mind to sit next to her each Saturday.

Mrs. Wills was particularly mean to the last guy, because he slipped in as she was locking the door. "We are now closed," she said to him.

"Sorry – I had to get a ride here," he said. He looked scruffy, but there was intelligence behind his eyes, and independence. He certainly didn't look cowed by Mrs. Wills. I admired him for that.

Mrs. Wills' friends glared at him as coldly as they could and thrust a hastily assembled box of food upon him. A package of moldy hot dog rolls topped the offering. He started to hand it back, saying "Thanks a lot. I can't use these, though."

Mrs. Wills pushed him out the door, squashing the rolls back into his box. "If you come here, yes you can," she said, shutting it in his face.

Eleanor looked disgusted. "Susan, you can see the green mold on the sides of those rolls from ten feet away!" she said.

Mrs. Wills just answered, "Perhaps that will motivate him to get a job."

I distinctly heard Eleanor mutter that he had a very low-paying one.

It was over, so I said good-bye and walked out.

Two other stragglers were getting into their cars. They looked miserable, but I couldn't tell much else just by looking at them. I wasn't about to judge just by appearances, but it would be interesting to imagine their lives and then, perhaps over time, learn how much was correct and how much wasn't.

Mrs. Wills came up behind me and said, "Next time you come, wear something a little better than that outfit. You look too much like the people who come here for food."

I stared back at her, shocked, but kept my mouth from dropping open. Whom were we supposed to impress? The poor people? Their situations seemed to be more than impressed upon them from what I had witnessed in the past hour – they seemed to be imprinted upon them. How could they ever forget Mrs. Wills and her friends? No wonder I didn't like their daughters. They were horrible people.

Mr. Baker came out just then and said, "Susan, Delphine is dressed exactly the way she ought to be dressed. Casual pants and a plain tee shirt are fine. The people who come here might be wearing suits and dresses for who knows what reason."

Mrs. Wills smiled tightly and said, "Of course, Mr. Baker. We want to make those people feel at ease." She glared at me.

I quickly said good-bye and went home.

The next week went the same, except that I slipped out of Elephant's Kitchen at precisely eleven o'clock so as to avoid interacting with Mrs. Wills. I had actually enjoyed sitting with Eleanor, and told my parents so at lunch.

"Well, I'm glad it's going well there," was all that my mother said.

My father just listened, and then showed me the summer organ recital list.

The third week, I had to use the bathroom halfway through the time. The bathroom was in the church, so I had to leave Elephant's Kitchen and go outside. As I got up, I heard Mrs. Wills mutter under her breath to the woman next to her, Erin's mother.

"These two are certainly well dressed to be coming here."

The woman in front of her table flushed a deep red, and tears formed in her eyes, but she managed to hold them in. She was wearing casual clothing that looked like it had been bought at the mall. It was in good condition; her blue blouse was quite pretty.

I walked outside and hid around the corner as the woman in the blue shirt emerged, and was appalled to see that Mrs. Wills had indeed made her cry. An older man in work boots came up to the door and spoke to her.

"Don't let them get you down, dear. They love doing this. Just don't come at the end – then they really focus on you. By then, they've had enough of poor people."

The woman just cried some more.

"Come on, you can get away from here now that you got the food," he said, trying to soothe her.

"But I will have to come again…probably. I've never had to do this before. I just lost my job – downsized and outsourced to India or someplace where they can get someone to do what I did for a fraction of what they paid me!" she wailed. "Life just isn't worth the effort if I can't keep a job that I studied for and worked hard at."

She ran to her car, threw her box of food in, and drove away, sobbing.

I felt angry, then very tired, and not from sleepiness. It was because I was angry and couldn't help. Katie's father had talked about cutting costs this way last Sunday over tea and scones in the church parlor. Frank Wills loved to take his cost-cutting savings and apply them to Republican Party efforts, and was equally fond of mentioning this.

Now that the coast was clear, I went to the bathroom and back, wondering how, if possible, I could have done better with that situation. Should I have come out to speak to that woman? Probably not; she might have felt spied upon and angry. And what words could a fourteen-year-old kid offer an adult that would be well-received, I wondered? Probably none; apparently my role was to be an observer. I hoped that there was some greater purpose to that.

On Wednesday night, when Nana brought the finished costumes to Ms. Hathaway and took me home with her for dinner, I asked her why she thought women like Mrs. Wills ran places like Elephant's Kitchen. The answer was interesting.

"I suppose women who have never had to work feel as though they ought to do something to justify their great good luck. I guess it makes them feel good. I wouldn't know, though. I had to work at the fabric store to supplement your grandfather's income, and help send your mother and aunt to college."

Nana took some cinnamon pie cookies out of the oven and picked up the newspaper again. "Oh, this is terrible."

"What is?"

"It's an obituary about a young woman who just lost her job. It was outsourced to a developing country, to someone who could do her work for less. She had put herself through college and gone to work on time for several years. She seemed, at least to her friends and family, to be coping well, but she killed herself Saturday afternoon."

There was a photo with the obituary. It was of the woman who had cried outside of Elephant's Kitchen before getting into her car and driving away.

I felt sick suddenly, and choked on my pie cookies as I tried to eat them.

"Are you all right, dear?" my

grandmother fussed.

"Yeah…I just have a headache. I need to lie down, I think."

Nana took me home.

As we drove off, I thought about what my grandmother had said, especially the part about meanness making someone feel good. Did it really? If so, what was wrong with Mrs. Wills?

And I hated the fact that one of the things I was learning was that I had to watch helplessly as life destroyed a nice person. I was a kid; I couldn't help that woman recover or replace her job, and I couldn't even contact her. I hadn't even had a clue as to what to say to her when I saw her crying.

The next evening, I asked my mother to tell me some more about Mrs. Wills.

My mother looked up from the food processor and cookbook, scooping pesto sauce into a bowl. "Susan Wills? I first met her and her parents when your father took me to meet his parents at the country club. She was there with her parents; they spent a lot of time at the clubhouse. Your grandparents practically threw your father at her right in front of me, but he ignored them." She smiled to herself. I smiled too.

"But what was she like, Mom?"

"Oh, rich, comfortable, clueless about other ways of life outside of the mall, the country club and the beauty parlor. I talked to her for a few minutes about art and music, the usual stuff. She wasn't into it, so I let her talk about her new clothes for a few minutes and made my escape. It was kind of funny. Your father and my parents thought it was ridiculous and hilarious…but don't you ever repeat this to anyone," she warned me.

She tended to add that admonishment to a lot of things that she told me, like a blanket of protection against social gaffes on my part. It was a good idea; I was only careful if I knew that something was a secret. Sensing that something shouldn't be shared with random other people was not one of my strong points. These warnings seemed to take care of that pitfall for me, for the most part.

My mother and I specialized in looking nice without making a huge production out of it. We went to a chic salon in town, but only to have our long hair trimmed. That was about it. No wonder my father liked my mother; she was a musician, she cooked and baked, she knew musical history, and so she had more interesting things to think and talk about than looks.

Back at Elephant's Kitchen on Saturday, I found myself watching Mrs. Wills and remembering Nana's casual analysis of her. Just like an elephant, Mrs. Wills seemed to remember everyone who came through the establishment, down to the last earring, threadbare tie, or…today it was a designer dress.

As I watched Mrs. Wills coldly and pointedly stare at a woman's designer dress, looking it up and down before starting to prepare her box of food, I was forcibly reminded of Mr. Baker's admonition that dress was no surefire indication of wealth or poverty. Who knew why people wore what they wore, anyway? Mrs. Wills acted like a telepath who had just invaded someone's mind and stolen information about this woman's life, then judged her harshly for it.

I couldn't wait to get out of here today. I was going to the mall with Nicole and Ariel, and looking forward to it. We would meet at one o'clock, and Ariel's mother would drive us to the mall. Thoughts of raspberry sorbet kept me occupied as Eleanor and I filled box after box, smiling for every glare meted out by the Wills Gang. At last it was over and I headed home to eat lunch and get ready to go. Exams and final papers were done; the Havermeyer School was to have a week of social activities before summer break. Let the fun begin…sort of. At least I could get more sleep at night, and write a bit.

At one o'clock, I joined my friends in Mrs. Fontaine's car, and we caught up on the news of the past twenty hours or so since we had last seen each other. I had described the Wills Gang, Elephant's Kitchen, and Eleanor to them before, so all I had to do was mention the woman in the designer dress and how Mrs. Wills had treated her.

Mrs. Fontaine was listening as she drove. "I wonder why she was wearing that dress; it could be for some reason other than fun," was all she would say.

We went into the mall and wasted no time in getting the fruit sorbets. Now that it was June, it quite warm out, so the cold treats felt great. We ate quickly and started wandering in and out of the stores.

When we came to a store that sold designer clothing, I couldn't believe my eyes. It looked like someone – or maybe everyone – had hit the jackpot in some perverse sort of lottery.

There, behind the counter, wearing her designer dress, was the woman who had gotten food at Elephant's Kitchen this morning. To top it all off, Mrs. Wills suddenly walked in right behind us, oblivious to everyone around her, scanning the racks of merchandise.

I dragged my friends behind one of the racks and quickly and quietly told them who each of the women was and what had occurred earlier.

Nicole looked like Christmas had come early. "I've got an idea. Stay just out of that clerk's sight, but get Mrs. Wills within earshot of the counter as fast as you can, and don't let her leave."

Ariel looked alarmed. "What are you going to do?"

I said, "I think I know. You'll love it if

it works." I was wondering if I would ever be able to face the Wills Gang on my own afterwards. Oh well, this will be so worth it, I thought.

Nicole walked right up to the counter and loudly addressed the woman behind it, "I love your dress! Do they require that employees wear the clothes that are sold here?"

Mrs. Wills glanced up, and recognized the woman from this morning.

Ariel and I stood in the doorway, blocking the exit.

Mrs. Wills looked back at us, then at the counter. The clerk recognized her, too. I stared coldly at Mrs. Wills, hoping that I was bringing it off as pointedly and coldly as the expert herself.

The clerk realized what was happening and replied, as if on cue, "Yes. They give us a discount, but we have to buy outfits here for work, and keep buying them. Last season's merchandise is not allowed. Just about all of my clothes are from here, and they aren't even tax deductible."

"That's terrible," I said. "It must eat up a significant chunk of your pay," and glared at Mrs. Wills as I said this. Mrs. Wills glared back.

"It does," the clerk answered. "I can pay bills, but then I need more money for food, and I just don't have it."

"Terrific," I said, in a tone that made it clear that I meant just the opposite.

I stepped away from the door, and Mrs. Wills left the store without a backward glance, looking livid.

It was worth it – for once, I felt good about a challenging interaction.

That night at dinner, I told my parents – and Nana, who was visiting – everything that I had experienced at Elephant's Kitchen, including the suicide and today's encounter at the mall. When I was finished, I expected to be in trouble for being rude to Mrs. Wills, but I was so mad that I just didn't care.

"I feel like something could go horribly wrong when I grow up and try to earn a living, and that I could end up getting food there, or at a place like it, and I would hate to be treated the way the Wills Gang – I mean Mrs. Wills and her friends – treat poor people."

Nana started laughing. "The Wills Gang...I love it. They deserve that name. But I do hope you haven't been going around saying that elsewhere," she added sternly.

"No, I've just been thinking it. This is the first time it's actually slipped out."

My parents glanced at each other, and then Dad said, "Well, we're proud of you, Delphine."

"That's a relief. I thought I was in trouble."

"Trouble?!" my mother looked amazed. "You were polite while making your opinions known. I knew you didn't want to give up sleeping late on Saturdays, but you did it anyway. Good. You have learned a lot, and if you don't want to go back, that's fine."

"I don't want to go back."

"That's fine."

"No, it's not."

My parents and grandmother exchanged glances.

"What do you intend to do, then?" they wanted to know.

"I really don't know, because some things are bothering me."

"What things?" her mother asked.

I thought for a moment. "I don't think I could spend time working with Mrs. Wills anymore. I mean, she's sure to tell her friends that I'm a horrible kid and have them all glare at me if I go back and just be so unpleasant that I'll hate it there for my own reasons. But if I quit, Eleanor will be the only person there who ever smiles at the poor people and treats them like worthwhile human beings. And I don't know what I might do – something nice for other people – instead of this. I need to think of something. That's what bothers me the most, but I don't know what to do about it."

"I see," my mother said, "and I'm glad

you feel that way. You can help me collect
food to drop off. Then you won't have quit,
and you can still see Eleanor. She will be
glad to stop meeting me at the gourmet
grocery stores to collect and carry stuff. And
next year, at school assemblies, you can
announce that you are collecting clothes to
donate. Students can drop them off at the
head's office, and you can get them each
week. You and I will bring them to a place
in Hartford."

My father added, "If Mr. Baker knows
half of what you've just told us, I'll be very
surprised…especially since he seems to use
the time that that place is open to write
sermons. It doesn't sound like he makes sure
that what he preaches is practiced by his – I
won't say listeners…"

"…churchgoers?" I offered.

"Exactly," my father replied. "It's only
seven o'clock. I'm going to call him."

I was horrified. "Why, Dad?"

He smiled. "So you won't have just
walked away from this without trying to
really help those unfortunate poor people."
He picked up the phone and started

punching in Mr. Baker's number.

A minute went by, then Dad said, "Cassie! How are you? Can you and Phil come over now for dessert? My family really needs to tell you something before tomorrow." There was a pause while Mrs. Baker checked with her husband. "Great – see you in a few minutes."

He hung up the phone and grinned. "Alyssa, do you have enough dessert?"

"A whole strawberry tart." She grinned back at him.

The minister and his wife came over, sat down at the kitchen table with us, and listened while my parents and grandmother made me tell them everything that I had just told them. I left no gory detail out.

"And I know I'll still see Eleanor at the pastry shop, but I felt bad about just leaving Elephant's Kitchen and never saying a word about how horrible the people who go there must be feeling when they get back into their cars, or walk home, or whatever they do next," I concluded.

The minister had listened gravely to the

entire tale. He was silent for a few minutes, then he said, "Delphine, I appreciate you telling me this, and I won't blame you for leaving. I think I will have to revise the sermon I prepared for tomorrow."

I must have still looked worried, because he spoke again.

"Oh, don't worry, Delphine," Mr. Baker said, "you can rest assured that Susan Wills and her friends will know why you left."

Now I really looked horrified at him; my eyes had widened a lot.

He smiled at me. "That's what happens when you stand up for other people. The ones you stand up to will resent you for it. Consider it a badge of honor, just so that it doesn't worry you or let them make you nervous. But don't talk about it with Mrs. Wills again. I know about your past history with her daughter, so you just leave this up to me."

"It's really my responsibility, now that I know what's been going on. I'm glad you told me – and I'll have to find a different hour in which to write sermons," he added ruefully.

"Mr. Baker – what are you going to do?" I couldn't resist the urge to ask.

"Well, Delphine, that's the awkward part of this – Mrs. Wills and her husband give a lot of money to St. Anne's Church. I don't want to be rude to them, but then again, I can't allow this to go on. I am going to have to involve myself more heavily and prominently in Elephant's Kitchen, and get to know the people who get food from it. I need to make sure that they go away feeling better – not worse – than they did when they arrived. That is how charitable work should be done. That is what my sermon tomorrow will be about."

I actually smiled at him. He hadn't used his booming tone of voice all evening.

Cassandra Baker promised to come to Elephant's Kitchen and sit with Eleanor, and explain what had happened at the mall when she could talk to her away from everyone else. She also said that she would make sure that people felt calm and hopeful before carrying their food boxes away.

I picked up my cat and went up to my room that night feeling much better than I had in a month. I had my Saturdays back, the poor people wouldn't be in tears at Elephant's Kitchen, and I would never forget the lessons I had learned from Mrs. Wills.

And I had some future plans for nice things to do for people on my own.

That was the best part – that, and the fact that I could sleep again, control my schedule, and enjoy a whole summer in which to write and practice the violin.

I just wished there would be no pressure to find a boyfriend. With Elephant's Kitchen out of the foreground, my mother was talking about the end-of-the year dance and Field Day, a day in which the whole school would spend time outside, signing yearbooks, picnicking, and playing with Frisbees.

If I didn't think I would have to report back about boys, it would have been fun.

It turned out that I worried for nothing.

Ariel and Nicole and I did play with a Frisbee, walk around the campus barefoot carrying our shoes, and eat too much watermelon and strawberry ice cream. We got our yearbooks signed by our teachers and by some kids in upper years, and by some foreign students (who were always interesting to talk to).

And the dance, though it was loud as usual, making conversation difficult, wasn't so bad. It was intriguing to watch how most of the other kids got hyped up by loud music and flashing lights. Sure, I had a few favorite rock songs, but I was an awkward dancer. Halfway through, I walked outside into the night air and sat down on a bench to enjoy some quiet time with no flashing lights in my eyes.

I heard the rustle of pages turning, and looked down the path at the next bench.

A boy from my history class was sitting with a large, dark, hard-cover book. He was cute, with short, straight, dark hair, and round, wire-rimmed glasses that reminded me of Harry Potter's, except that they were in a perfect state of repair. His name was Joel Shriner, and he was a quiet kid in my year. I hadn't spoken to him much before.

I usually avoided boys because I didn't want crushes or any upsets associated with them to distract me from my work. That wasn't the only reason; most boys made a lot of noise and loved team sports. I had too little in common with them. But this boy was different. He rarely spoke, and was usually on his own, surrounded by books in the library. The athletic boys treated him the way that Katie and her clique treated me.

Fortunately, none of those boys or girls were anywhere in sight; they were busy doing slow dances in the gym, clinging to each other as if they would get married even though that was doubtful.

Joel was a polite enough boy, but I had resisted the urge to get to know him and done my work, memorized my lines in the play, and practiced my violin music.

But work was over with for the next three months.

"Why do you have a book with you in the dark?" I called over to him.

Joel looked up. "The dance is too loud, and I'd rather read. Why are you out here?"

"Same reason as you are; what's the book?"

"*The Star Trek Compendium*," he said.

"I love that book!" I said. "My father gave it to me for Christmas!"

Joel grinned. "Not too many girls like *Star Trek*," he remarked.

I grinned back, held up my hand in the Vulcan ta'al position, and replied, "Peace and long life; live long and prosper."

"You can do that?" He looked delighted.

"Yeah," I said. "And Dr. McCoy can't."

"Come over here," he said.

I did, and we chatted until the dance ended. He told me that he wanted to study physics, get his Ph.D., and work in Switzerland at CERN someday on nuclear fusion and the god particle. We even made eye contact a few times...and could actually read something as we did so. I think it might have been happiness at finding a new friend who was more than just a friend.

"By the way," Joel said, halfway

through the evening, "nice save with Katie when she forgot her lines in the play."

I grinned; Katie had written her lines all over her hand, draped a handkerchief over it, and then lost her place during the first performance. I had skipped ahead until she remembered what to say. And Joel had attended all three performances!

We exchanged e-mail addresses, phone numbers, and addresses.

My mother would be pleased, I thought.

Joel gave me a kiss on the cheek before I left with Ariel and Nicole, but I didn't tell my parents that. At least, not right away…

About the Author

Stephanie C. Fox, J.D. is a historian, author, and editor. She is a graduate of William Smith College and the University of Connecticut School of Law. She runs an editing service called *QueenBeeEdit*, found at www.queenbeeedit.com, which caters to politicians, scientists, and others.

Ms. Fox has written several books on a variety of topics, including the effects of human overpopulation on the environment, Asperger's, cats, and travel to Kuwait and Hawai'i.

www.ingramcontent.com/pod-product-compliance
Lightning Source LLC
Chambersburg PA
CBHW071013120726
47910CB00004B/1500